John,
Enjoy reading all
about dinosaurs!
Love.
Aunt Tina
November 2, 2018

D1307114

DID DINOSAURS HAVE DENTISTS?

by Patrick O'Donnell

Illustrated by Erik Mehlen

To my sons, who are a constant source of light and inspiration, and to everyone who encouraged me along the way, I offer my heartfelt thanks.

– PATRICK O'DONNELL

To Ava Claire Bear and Weezy Louise.

— ERIK MEHLEN

DID DINOSAURS HAVE DENTISTS?

DID A TRICERATOPS USE A TOOTHPICK?

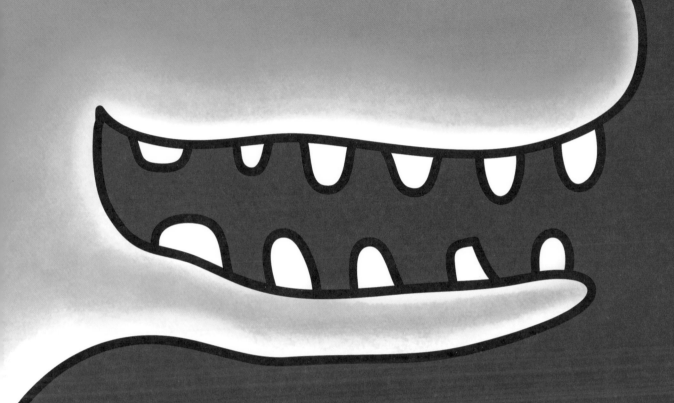

DID A MEGALOSAURUS'S
MOLARS NEED CLEANING

AFTER A PREHISTORIC PICNIC?

DID A CAMARASAURUS

EVER GET A

CROWN?

DID A STEGOSAURUS
LIKE TO

FLOSS

OR DID IT MAKE HIM FROWN?

IF A TYRANNOSAURUS USED TOOTHPASTE

WOULD IT LEAVE THE TUBE ALL SQUASHED?

DID A DIPLODOCUS

EVER GET DENTURES?

DID A PTERODACTYL

DID A BABY BACTROSAURUS
BRUSH LONG ENOUGH

OR DID
IT RUN
AND
HIDE?

THESE ARE THE QUESTIONS I THINK OF

WHEN DAD SAYS IT'S TIME FOR ME

TO VISIT OUR FAMILY DENTIST

AND GET CHECKED FOR CAVITIES.

ONE TIME I ASKED THE HYGIENIST

AND SHE ANSWERED IN A BLINK:

Triceratops (try-sare-uh-tops): This plant-eater's name means "three-horned face." It had a really big head, with 3 horns that were about 3 feet long and a frill — the bony part that protected its neck — that could be up to 7 feet wide!

Megalosaurus (meg-uh-low-sawr-us): When your name means "big lizard," you probably won't get bullied. In fact, it's likely the other dinosaurs tried to stay far away, since they were on the menu: this 12-foot-tall dino ate meat. Despite the name, megalosaurus was far from the biggest dinosaur.

Brachiosaurus (brack-ee-oh-sawr-us): This giant seems much more deserving of the name "big lizard" than megalosaurus: It stood 50 feet tall, was 100 feet long, and weighed about 120,000 pounds! Its name, however, means "arm lizard" — go figure! Brachiosaurus ate plants.

Camarasaurus (come-air-ah-sawr-us): The name means "chambered lizard" and refers to the fact that it had hollow spaces, or chambers, in its spine. This plant eater probably traveled in packs.

Stegosaurus (steg-uh-sawr-us): A plant eater, stegosaurus's name means "roof lizard." Not because it liked to climb on roofs, but because it took its own roof along wherever it went: It had large, triangular plates all along its back. It also had a spiky tail, so other dinosaurs didn't mess with it.

Centrosaurus (sen-truh-sawr-us): This plant-eating dino had 1 big horn above its nose, and its name means "pointed lizard." It had a beak-like mouth and traveled in packs. Like the triceratops, this dino had a frill around its neck.

Microraptor (mike-row-rap-tour): This was the smallest dinosaur, at about 17 inches long and weighing only about 3 pounds! It was covered in feathers and had FOUR wings! Scientists think this meat-eater hunted at night.

Tyrannosaurus (tie-ran-uh-sawr-us): This meat-eater's name means "tyrant lizard." "Tyrant" is another word for "mean." It was 23 feet tall, had a huge head, and had teeth that were about 7 inches long! Scientists think it could run pretty fast in short bursts, and although it had tiny arms, they were really strong.

Diplodocus (di-plod-uh-cuss): At 30 feet tall, it was easy for this dinosaur to reach the plants it liked to eat. Its name means "double beam," because it had two rows of bones in its tail to provide support. It's thought to be one of the longest dinosaurs — from nose to tip of tail, it measured about 90 feet!

Pterodactyl (terr-uh-dack-tull): This "dinosaur" isn't technically considered a dinosaur at all — scientists say it's a pterosaur, which is a fancy way of saying "flying reptile." Its wings are really four-fingered hands, and that fourth finger was really long and stretched to the end of its wing.

Bactrosaurus (back-tro-sawr-us): Like a platypus, this plant eater had a duck-shaped bill on its face. The bill was toothless, but it had teeth farther back in its mouth, near its cheeks. Its name means "club-spined lizard," because it had spines on its back.

Our teeth are important for more than just eating — they also help us to speak clearly. Doctors have found that taking good care of our teeth also leads to better overall health! Here are some common dental terms.

ORAL HYGIENE GLOSSARY

BRACES: Special brackets that are used to straighten crooked teeth. They can make your smile look even nicer than it already does — but more importantly, they help make your mouth healthier by helping to prevent tooth decay, tooth loss, and other problems that can be caused by crooked teeth.

CAVITIES: Holes in your teeth usually caused by not brushing or flossing properly. A cavity can first break through a tooth's outer layer, called "enamel," and then a tooth's inner layer, called "dentin." Cavities weaken your teeth and can lead to other health problems, too.

CROWN: A type of cover or filling used to repair a tooth. Crowns can fix a chipped or broken tooth or make a tooth stronger to keep it from breaking.

DENTIST: A doctor who specializes in helping you take care of your teeth and gums (the part of your mouth that surrounds your teeth).

DENTURES: A set of removable fake teeth that are used to replace missing teeth. Just like your natural teeth, they need to be brushed!

FLOSS: String that's used to get between your teeth to remove bits of food and plaque (a sticky substance that can cause cavities) your toothbrush couldn't reach.

FLUORIDE: A mineral that helps prevent cavities by making your teeth stronger.

HYGIENIST: An expert who works with your dentist to make sure your teeth and gums are healthy. Hygienists have a lot of jobs, including cleaning your teeth, looking for signs of cavities and other problems in your mouth, and giving you tips on taking care of your teeth.

MOLARS: The teeth at the back of your mouth, used for grinding up food. You also have incisors at the front of your mouth for grabbing, cutting, tearing, and holding food; and canines, which are pointy and also are used for cutting and tearing food.

MOUTHWASH: A liquid used to rinse out your mouth and get rid of the bacteria that cause bad breath and cavities.

TOOTHPASTE: A paste, gel, or powder that's used with your toothbrush to clean your teeth.

BIBLIOGRAPHY

The following online sources were used to clarify some of
the names, pronunciations, and facts about the dinosaurs in
this book:

DinoDictionary.com: www.dinodictionary.com
Dinosaur Pictures and Facts: www.dinosaurpictures.org
Encyclopedia Britannica: www.britannica.com
The Natural History Museum's DinoDirectory.com:
      www.nhm.ac.uk/discover/dino-directory/index.html
Oral Hygiene Glossary:
      www.britannica.com
      www.mouthhealthy.org

PATRICK O'DONNELL HAS BEEN WRITING STORIES SINCE HE WAS EIGHT YEARS OLD, AND HE'S ONLY EVER HAD TWO CAVITIES. HE'S HELD MANY JOBS, INCLUDING COPY EDITOR, COOK, LANDSCAPER, PHOTOGRAPHER, AND EVEN SMALL-ENGINE MECHANIC, BUT HIS FAVORITE TWO JOBS ARE WRITER AND FATHER. HIS TWO BOYS USED TO BE AFRAID OF THE DENTIST, BUT THEY LOVE TO VISIT NOW. THEY ALSO LOVE, IN NO PARTICULAR ORDER, DINOSAURS, SPAGHETTI AND MEATBALLS, LEAVING LAUNDRY AND LEGOS ALL OVER THE FLOOR, AND STORY TIME.

RAISED BY WOLVES IN THE DEEP JUNGLES OF INDIA AFTER A TIGER ATTACK SEPARATED HIM FROM HIS FAMILY . . . WAIT A MINUTE, WRONG BIO. OKAY, HERE WE GO: ERIK MEHLEN IS AN ILLUSTRATOR WHO HAS RECEIVED AWARDS FROM THE SOCIETY OF ILLUSTRATORS. HE STUDIED AT ATLANTA COLLEGE OF ART AND LIVES IN SAN ANTONIO, TEXAS.

Library of Congress Control Number: 2018934609

Designed by Patrick O'Donnell and Erik Mehlen
Illustrated by Erik Mehlen
Art Direction and Layout by Danielle D. Farmer
Cover design by Brenda McCallum
Type set in original typography by Erik Mehlen/Fontoon/Avenir LT Std

ISBN: 978-0-7643-5602-5
Printed in Hong Kong

Published by Schiffer Publishing, Ltd.
4880 Lower Valley Road
Atglen, PA 19310
Phone: (610) 593-1777; Fax: (610) 593-2002
E-mail: Info@schifferbooks.com
Web: www.schifferbooks.com

For our complete selection of fine books on this and related subjects, please visit our website at www.schifferbooks.com. You may also write for a free catalog.

Schiffer Publishing's titles are available at special discounts for bulk purchases for sales promotions or premiums. Special editions, including personalized covers, corporate imprints, and excerpts, can be created in large quantities for special needs. For more information, contact the publisher.

We are always looking for people to write books on new and related subjects. If you have an idea for a book, please contact us at proposals@schifferbooks.com.